SIMON PUTTOCK was born in New Zealand and now lives in Edinburgh. He studied English Literature at Newcastle University and has written many picture books including *The Thing* (illustrated by Daniel Egnéus), the Moonlight School series (illustrated by Ali Pye) and *The Baby That Roared* (illustrated by Nadia Shireen). Simon has been a judge for the Whitbread Children's Award and the Kathleen Fidler Award, and a guest lecturer in picture books at the University of Newcastle-upon-Tyne.

MATT ROBERTSON began to draw and paint as soon as he was old enough to pick up a paintbrush. When he reached the age of 18 he set off to University to study Illustration at the Cambridge School of Art. It was here that his love for picture books grew. In 2014 he won the Lara Jones award for 'Blankets' and also won second prize in the Macmillan Book Prize for the same book. His first picture book, *Super Stan* – published by Orchard Books April 2016 – was nominated for the Waterstones Children's Book Prize 2017.

First published in 2017 by Lincoln Children's Books
First published in paperback in 2018 by Lincoln Children's Books
an imprint of The Quarto Group.
The Old Brewery, 6 Blundell Street, London N7 9BH, United Kingdom.
T (0)20 7700 6700 F (0)20 7700 8066 **www.QuartoKnows.com**

A catalogue record for this book is available from the British Library.

ISBN 978-1-78603-094-8

The illustrations were created with mixed media
Set in American Typewriter

Published by Rachel Williams
Designed by Karissa Santos
Edited by Jenny Broom and Katie Cotton
Production by Jenny Cundill

Manufactured in Dongguan, China TL 092017

9 8 7 6 5 4 3 2 1

Frances Lincoln
Children's Books

Mr Moot lived all alone
with his beloved pet Fluffywuffy.

Mr Moot was not
troubled by mice.

He did not have noisy
neighbours.

And he hardly ever got
any letters delivered...

'I do like a nice, quiet life,' said Mr Moot.

Then one day, there was a knock at the door.

'I've come for a week,' said Cousin Clarence, 'or a month, or quite possibly a year!'

'Oh dear!' said Mr Moot. 'I mean, come in and make yourself at home. Meet Fluffywuffy!'

Cousin Clarence made himself at home immediately.

'I am very sleepy,' he declared, and he put himself to bed on the living room sofa.

'I don't suppose he'll be much bother,' said Mr Moot.

Fluffywuffy said nothing.

That night, Mr Moot was woken by a **noise**.

A **noise** of enormous proportions.

Whatever could it be?

Mr Moot switched on the living room light.
'Sometimes,' said Cousin Clarence,
'I just like a little night music.'

'Well, as long as it's
only sometimes,'
said Mr Moot, 'I expect
it won't be a bother.'

Fluffywuffy
said nothing.

The next night, Mr Moot was woken again, by another, quite different, but equally enormous **noise**. What could be happening **now**?

Mr Moot switched on
the living room light.

'Sometimes,' said Cousin Clarence, 'I just get the urge to make something.'

'As long as it's only sometimes, I suppose it's okay,' said Mr Moot. 'And as long as you're trying not to be a bother.'

'I most certainly am trying,' said Cousin Clarence happily.

Fluffywuffy said nothing.

But the **next** night, well! Mr Moot was woken by another enormous **noise**.

A noise that was almost impossible to describe.

Mr Moot switched on the living room light.

'Friday nights only!' said Cousin Clarence before Mr Moot could say a word. 'I find it very relaxing after a hard week.'

'Well **that's** all right then, I suppose,' said Mr Moot, who was having a bit of a hard week himself. 'After all, **next** Friday **is** seven days away.' Fluffywuffy said nothing.

Not very surprisingly, the next night, Mr Moot could not get to sleep. He lay awake, waiting for a noise to begin.

And after a while there was a noise: a noise entirely impossible to describe.

It was not the sound
of motorbikes...

or drums...

or circular
saws...

It was a noise
that got louder,
and louder
until suddenly—

SCRUNK!

(Perhaps the oddest noise
of all.) And then there was
complete and utter silence!

Mr Moot listened:
the silence
persisted.

He listened some more: the silence went on…
‘Perhaps,’ he said to himself in worried tones,
‘I had better go and see.’

Mr Moot switched on the living room light and...

Cousin Clarence
was not there!

'Gone!' said Mr Moot. 'Disappeared!
Without so much as a goodbye or a thank you!'

Fluffywuffy said nothing.

'Mind you,' said Mr Moot,
'isn't it lovely and quiet?'
Fluffywuffy said nothing.

‘Night night, Fluffywuffy!’ said Mr Moot, switching off the light. ‘Sleep tight!’

And Fluffywuffy smiled...
but Fluffywuffy said nothing.

MORE FUNNY STORIES FROM FRANCES LINCOLN CHILDREN'S BOOKS

The Cave
by Rob Hodgson

There is a cave.
A cave that is home to a creature.
A creature that never leaves its cave...
Because of a wolf.

The wolf tries everything to get the creature to leave the cave, to no avail. But what will happen when he's finally successful? This is a laugh-out-loud story with a BIG surprise!

978-1-84780-911-7
£11.99

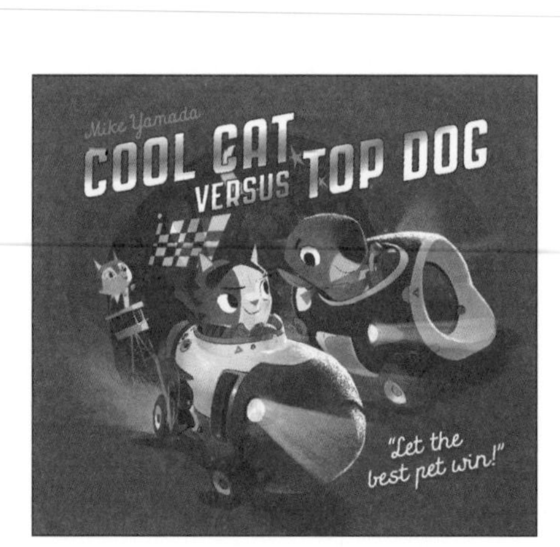

Cool Cat vs Top Dog
by Mike Yamada

The annual midnight race around the block, Pet Quest, is upon the neighbourhood. The rivalry between the two fastest kids on the block, Cool Cat and Top Dog, is reaching fever pitch, and to make matters worse, the two challengers live in the same household. Their competitiveness looks set to cost them the race – can they find a way to work together before all is lost?

978-1-84780-739-7
£6.99

Toad Has Talent
by Richard Smythe

Every year when Moonlight Pond freezes over, a talent contest takes place deep in the woods. Ducks dance, mice perform... However, there is one animal that never competes. Toad watches the talent show from behind his rock, careful to keep himself hidden. But this year, Toad might just discover that you never know what you can do until you try...

978-1-78603-011-5
£11.99